Sometimes I'm Afraid

Written by Maribeth Boelts

Illustrated by Cheri Bladholm

Zonderkidz

Zonderkidz®

The children's group of Zondervan

www.zonderkidz.com

Sometimes I'm Afraid
Copyright © 2004 by The Zondervan Corporation
Illustrations copyright © 2004 by Cheri Bladholm}

Requests for information should be addressed to:
Zonderkidz, *Grand Rapids, Michigan 49530*

Library of Congress Cataloging-in-Publication Data

Boelts, Maribeth, 1964-
  Sometimes I'm afraid : a book about fear / by Maribeth Boelts ; [illustrations by Cheri Bladholm]. –
1st ed.
    p. cm.
  Summary: Three different children are helped by caring adults to deal with frightful feelings through
prayer.
  ISBN 0-310-70657-2 (Hardcover)
  [1. Fear — Fiction. 2. Fear of the dark — Fiction. 3. Christian life — Fiction.] I. Title: Sometimes I
am afraid. II. Bladholm, Cheri, ill. III. Title. PZ7.B635744 So 2004 [E] – dc22
                                                                                    2003021480

Editor: Gwen Ellis
Art Direction & Design: Laura M. Maitner

Printed in China

05 06 07/ HK /4 3 2

IT WAS MORNING in the neighborhood where Jake, Nika, and Brandon lived.

"I'll never remember how to spell all the words on my spelling test," Jake said, poking at his scrambled eggs.

"Tests can feel kind of scary," Jake's mom said. "But we practiced each night this week, and last night, you got every word right."

"Yes, but that was just practice," Jake said. "This is a test! What if I can't remember any of the words? What if my teacher reads the list too fast?"

JAKE'S MOM LISTENED. "You know," she said, "sometimes I feel scared the way you do right now."

"Like you don't want to take a spelling test?" Jake asked.

"Well, not exactly," said his mom, smiling. "But other stuff scares me. Say, Jake, have you prayed about your test or asked God to help you?"

"Not exactly," replied Jake.

"How about I walk you to the bus stop—we can pray on the way," said his mom.

As Jake and his mom walked, she prayed, "God, you are Jake's help and his place of safety. Please be with him as he takes his spelling test, and strengthen him when he feels afraid."

Jake let his mom's prayer sink in. Just as the bus rounded the corner, Jake felt God's presence with him. All of a sudden he knew.

"I think I can do it," Jake said. "I think I can remember my spelling words."

"I think you can, too," his mom replied.

As the sun set over the neighborhood, Nika yawned. She shut her closet door and told herself that inside her closet were five stuffed bears, eight puzzles, six half-used coloring books, a pair of Rollerblades, and a big bucket of seashells. After pulling her covers up tight, Nika stared at her closet door. Suddenly she was sure she saw monsters. She was sure she heard monsters. She was even sure she smelled monsters.

"GRANDMA!" she called, trembling.

"THERE ARE NO MONSTERS allowed here," Grandma said. Grandma found a night light with three stars and a golden moon. She plugged it in and sat down on Nika's bed. Together, they sang some of their favorite songs from church. Soon, the little room was filled with soft light and soft music—and absolutely no monsters.

As Grandma's lips brushed Nika's forehead with a kiss, she said, "God helps heal scary thoughts." Nika nodded her head and agreed, though when it came to monsters in the closet, Nika needed Grandma to remind her.

LATE THAT NIGHT, while Nika and Jake dreamed, a storm rolled in. Thunder rumbled and rattled the house, and lightning flashed through Brandon's bedroom window. A branch, tossed by the wind's muscle, scraped against the side of the house. As the rain raced to build puddles, Brandon's heart pounded with fear.

"STORMS COME," Brandon's dad said, hugging him close. "But they move on, too." Then he prayed. "Father, you love and care for us, and tonight, Brandon is afraid. Please calm Brandon's heart. Help him feel your love and your strong arms of protection around him through this stormy night."

BRANDON AND DAD listened together, and soon the wind eased and the grumble of thunder sounded farther and farther away. Brandon's head grew heavy, and he rested it on his dad's shoulder. After a while, the only sound in the room was the sprinkling of rain on the windowpane and the slow, even breath of a sleeping Brandon.

As the neighborhood slept, God whispered a promise to Brandon, Nika, and Jake.

"I am with you," God said.

"I will help you."

"I love you."

"And no matter how much the world changes, I stay the same—forever."

And God whispers that promise to you today.

"So do not be afraid. I am with you. Do not be terrified. I am your God.
I will make you strong and help you. My powerful right hand will take good care of you."

(Isaiah 41:10)

WHEN YOUR CHILD IS AFRAID

This book focuses on a variety of fears children can have. Some fears are healthy fears. Fear of strangers that could hurt your child, fear of running out on a busy street, and fear of touching a hot stove are fears that serve them well. These fears help them deal with the world in a safer and healthier way.

Other fears, though understandable in a child's life, can create a problem for your child. Jake's fears kept him from doing his best. Nika's fears made the whole world a frightening place. And Brandon's fears made a natural and wonderful part of God's creation become a frightening event.

As you might have noticed, in each case the child had someone—Jakes' mom, Nika's grandma, and Brandon's dad—to offer reassurance. They did much more than try to logically explain away the children's fears. (Fears that create problems are not logical, they are psychological in nature.) When God reassures his people and says, "Be not afraid," he gives a reason, "for I am with you always."

It can be difficult to approach a child's fears. The child's fears may reflect your own. Sometimes we just don't know how to be reassuring. Take heart. Just being there to remind your child of your love and concern has a positive impact.

- Let your child know that it is natural to be afraid. Being afraid is part of life, a part that reminds us of our need to remember God's immense and eternal love for us.
- Remind yourself and your child that God understands why we are afraid better than we do. And he loves us no matter what.

- After you read this book, pray with your child. Pray for God to help your child with fears now and with fears he may have in the future. Thank God for loving you both, and thank God for the reminder that we are his children.
- Make a plan to help your child face his or her fears. Research in psychology indicates that gradually facing fears and practice in handling fears is the best way to reduce them. Jake's mom could help him by having him take practice spelling tests at home. Nika's grandma could help her draw a picture of God's angels around her protecting her at night. Brandon's dad could help him pretend to be in a noisy thunderstorm—all related enough to approach the fear in a gradual way.
- Take the time to be with your child and point out how you are reminded of God's presence in everyday life.
- Practice saying with your child, "I know this feels scary, but my parents love me, God is with me, and I know I will be safe."

Even if your child is not struggling with a fear at the present time, reading this book over and over will help "fear proof" your child.

A Word to Parents and Other Caregivers

Everyday life in God's world presents challenges and problems for all of us. Children, as well as adults, struggle with a variety of feelings when faced with emotionally charged situations. By helping our children clearly recognize God's loving presence in their lives—that he is with them no matter what happens—we help to prepare them for life. One of the names of Jesus Christ is "Emanuel, God with us," and God with us is the pervasive theme of this Helping Kids Heal series. The books honestly and sensitively address the difficult emotions children face.

Children love a good story, and stories can provide a safe way to approach issues, concerns, and problems. Therapists who work with children have long used stories to help children acknowledge emotions they would rather avoid. When a loving parent, a kind grandparent, or a caring teacher reads about a story character who is experiencing difficult feelings, the child has permission to feel, to ask questions, to voice his or her fears, and to struggle with emotions. Remember, as with any good story, one reading is never enough. Repetition is a great reminder of the truths contained in the story.

Each child is different. Some children, when facing a difficult emotion, will ask questions and wonder aloud about the characters in the books. Other children are content to just listen and take it all in. After several readings, try to draw them out to talk about the story. You, more than anyone else, will know what the child needs. Keep these things in mind as you use these books:

- God is with you, too. You may be reading about something that is close to your heart. Your emotions may be as tender as the child's as you read the story. Pray that you will have a sense of God's loving presence in your heart.

- You do not have to know the perfect answer for every question, nor do you have to answer all of the child's questions. Some of the best questions are the hardest to answer. Be sure, however, to acknowledge the child's question. Be honest. Say that you don't have the answer. If the child asks, "Why did she have to die?" it's all right to say, "I don't know."

- Pray with the child to feel God's loving presence. Let the child know that you care about him or her and about his or her feelings. Let the child know that whether he or she feels God's presence or not, God is still with him or her. This is a loving, precious, and powerful gift that you can give the child.

- Be aware that God works in a variety of ways. You may not get much of a response from the child as you read this book. Don't be concerned. Read the book at different times. You are planting a seed—a seed for the child to recognize God is at work in everyone's life.

- Have fun! Enjoy the story and this time with the child. Children are precious gifts from God created in his image. God is helping you to prepare the child for a future in his kingdom.

Dr. Scott

R. Scott Stehouwer, Ph.D., professor of psychology, Calvin College, and clinical psychologist